Fairy-Tale & Phonics

Sleeping Beauty

This book practices:

12 single sounds — also called phonemes

One letter forming one sound:

b (as in bell)   w (as in was)   k (as in king)
h (as in horse)   y (as in yet)   t (as in tale)

Two or more letters forming one sound:

ch (as in child)   th (as in them)

or (as in born) *also spelled -oor, -ore, -ar, -our*

oo (as in stool) *also spelled -o, -ou, -ew, -ue*

ee (as in deep) *also spelled -e, -ea*

ear (as in near)

5 blends — made by two consonant sounds

Two or more consonants are sounded out individually but are blended together:

ks (as in fox)   sp (as in spell)
br (as in brave)   cr (as in crown)   pr (as in prince)

How to use this book:

Read aloud and sound out the highlighted sounds on each page

Try the activities at the bottom of the page

Retell the story using the pictures and key sounds on page 23

Practice the sounds with the matching activity on page 24

Once upon a time, a baby girl was born to a king and queen. She was a beautiful child.

Say the words as you spot each thing beginning with b.

bow   baby   bell

The king beamed with happiness
and began planning a big party
to celebrate the birth.

Sound out these words beginning with the b sound.

band   bird   belt   bag
beach   bowl   bump

…ght the ks blend (as in fox) as you read

Excited visitors brought presents in colorful boxes.

Can you **see** six presents in the room?

The fairies were all invited too, except one who was extra mean and spiteful.

Spell some words with the ks blend.

fox   mix   wax   exit

When it was time, the fairies waved their wands and cast wonderful spells.

We wish you well!

Say the words as you spot each thing beginning with w.

woman   wand   wings

Just as the last sparkly spell was cast, there was a whoosh, and the spiteful fairy spun into the room!

Sound out these words with the sp blend.

spark   sport   spider   spent

space   spoon   speak

6

"This will spoil your fun!"
she laughed.

"The princess is special indeed!
One day she will prick her finger
on a spindle and fall down dead!"

Spell some more words beginning with sp.

sped   spot   spill   spy   spin

Focus on the k sound, made by c and k (as in king)

How cunning the mean fairy was! The queen collapsed into the king's arms.

"I cannot completely undo the curse," said a kind fairy. "The princess will prick her finger, but she will just fall asleep. Only a prince can wake her with a kiss."

Say the words as you spot each thing with the k sound.

curl   candle   king

The king immediately called for all the spindles in the country to be destroyed.

Sound out some more words with the k sound.

card   coat   keep   kind

bucket   kick   shock   back

Highlight the or sound (as in born) as you read

Many years later, the princess was exploring the castle when she saw a door she had not seen before.

Sound out these words, which all have the or sound.

born   fork   horn   fort

floor   more   score

Steps led to another door, so the princess thought she would go through and see more.

Her father had warned her about wandering off, but of course, the princess didn't listen.

Spell some more words with the or sound.

short   warm   corn   your

The princess walked up the steps into a spooky room.

An old woman was sitting on a stool. "What are you doing?" asked the princess.

Sound out these words with the oo sound.

moon   boot   do   too
grew   chew   blue   true

Focus on
the ch sound
(as in child)

"Watch, my child," said the old woman.
"I'm spinning — it's such fun. Why don't
I teach you?"

The princess stepped forward
to touch the spindle.

Spell some words with the ch sound.

chat   porch   peach   match

13

Emphasize
the ee sound
(as in deep)

As soon as she touched the spindle's needle,
the princess fell into a deep enchanted sleep.

"Time to flee!" said the old woman,
who was really the mean fairy.

Sound out these words with the ee sound.

me   be   tea   clean   seat

sweet   feet   tree

The king and queen also fell asleep.
Servants stopped cleaning and dozed off.

Even the pony fell asleep on his feet,
and the birds stopped tweeting!

Spell some more words with the ee sound.

meat   speak   green   sheet

Highlight
the ear sound
(as in near)

Years and years went by, and a huge
hedge of thorns began to appear around
the castle, so no one could get near it.

Spell some words with the ear sound.

clear   dear   fear   hear

One hundred years later, a handsome prince was hunting on his horse when he happened to see the turrets of the castle above the hedge.

Point to some things that begin with h.

Finish the sentence with the h sound.

"What is hidden behind here?"

Draw attention to the y sound (as in yet)

"Yoo-hoo!" yelled the prince as he hacked through the hedge.

It seemed to take years, yet he kept going.

"You are all so quiet," said the prince when he saw the young servants. "Oh, you're all asleep!"

Sound out these words, which all have the y sound.

yes   yelp   yard   yolk
yellow   your   yo-yo

18

Then the prince remembered the tale of a terrible curse, so he set off to find the sleeping princess.

He kissed her, and she opened her eyes straight away. It was love at first sight.

Are you all right?

Spell some words, which all use the t sound.

top   tall   tiny   boat   feet

19

As the prince and princess crept through the crumbling castle, they brought everyone back to life.

Say the names of the things with the br, cr, and pr blends, as you spot them.

brick   crown   prince   princess

The princess proudly presented the brave prince to her parents. The cruel fairy's spell had been broken forever!

Spell words with the br, cr, and pr blends.

bring   crab   cross   prop

Emphasize the hard th sound (as in them)

Sleeping Beauty and the prince were so happy to be together that they were soon married.

They lived happily ever after, and the mean fairy never bothered them again.

Sound out the words thin and they. Can you hear the difference?

Sound out these words with the hard th sound.

those   there   mother   brother

Try to **retell** the story using
these key sounds and story images.

baby

wand

spiteful

king

door

touch

sleep

handsome

together

Think of a word that matches
the red highlighted **sounds** on each line.

wax	mix	exit
stool	grew	blue
green	seat	clean
dear	hear	year
yard	yo-yo	you
tiny	set	feet
brick	broken	bring
crab	cross	cruel
princess	prop	proudly

You've had fun with phonics! Well done.

Published in 2018 by Windmill Books, an Imprint of Rosen Publishing, 29 East 21st Street, New York, NY 10010

Copyright © 2018 Miles Kelly Publishing

All rights reserved. No part of this book may be reproduced in any form without permission in writing from the publisher, except by a reviewer.

Publishing Director: Belinda Gallagher | Creative Director: Jo Cowan | Senior Editor: Fran Bromage | Designer: Jo Cowan
Phonics Consultant: Susan Purcell | Illustrator: Rosie Butcher | Concept: Fran Bromage
Acknowledgments: The publishers would like to thank the following sources for the use of their photographs: t = top, b = bottom, rt = repeated throughout.
Cover graphic (t, b) tomka/Shutterstock, (rt) DeepGreen/iStock, (rt) koya979/Shutterstock, (rt) solarbird/Shutterstock

Cataloging-in-Publication Data
Names: Purcell, Susan.
Title: Sleeping beauty / Susan Purcell.
Description: New York : Windmill Books, 2018. | Series: Fairy-tale phonics | Includes index.
Identifiers: ISBN 9781508194491 (pbk.) | ISBN 9781508193784 (library bound) | ISBN 9781508194552 (6 pack)
Subjects: LCSH: Sleeping Beauty (Tale) -- Juvenile fiction. | Reading--Phonetic method--Juvenile fiction.
Classification: LCC PZ7.P834 Sl 2018 | DDC [F]--dc23
Manufactured in the United States of America
CPSIA Compliance Information: Batch BW18WM: For Further Information contact Rosen Publishing, New York, New York at 1-800-237-9932